# Dear Parents:

Congratulations! Your child is taking the first steps on an exciting journey. The destination? Independent reading!

**STEP INTO READING®** will help your child get there. The program offers five steps to reading success. Each step includes fun stories and colorful art or photographs. In addition to original fiction and books with favorite characters, there are Step into Reading Non-Fiction Readers, Phonics Readers and Boxed Sets, Sticker Readers, and Comic Readers—a complete literacy program with something to interest every child.

## Learning to Read, Step by Step!

### Ready to Read    Preschool–Kindergarten
• big type and easy words • rhyme and rhythm • picture clues
For children who know the alphabet and are eager to begin reading.

### Reading with Help    Preschool–Grade 1
• basic vocabulary • short sentences • simple stories
For children who recognize familiar words and sound out new words with help.

### Reading on Your Own    Grades 1–3
• engaging characters • easy-to-follow plots • popular topics
For children who are ready to read on their own.

### Reading Paragraphs    Grades 2–3
• challenging vocabulary • short paragraphs • exciting stories
For newly independent readers who read simple sentences with confidence.

### Ready for Chapters    Grades 2–4
• chapters • longer paragraphs • full-color art
For children who want to take the plunge into chapter books but still like colorful pictures.

**STEP INTO READING®** is designed to give every child a successful reading experience. The grade levels are only guides; children will progress through the steps at their own speed, developing confidence in their reading.

Remember, a lifetime love of reading starts with a single step!

FROSTY THE SNOWMAN and all related characters and elements © & ™ Warner Bros.
Entertainment Inc. and Classic Media, LLC. Based on the musical composition FROSTY
THE SNOWMAN © Warner/Chappell Music, Inc. (s17)

RHUS39292

Visit us on the Web!
StepIntoReading.com
randomhousekids.com

Educators and librarians, for a variety of teaching tools, visit us at RHTeachersLibrarians.com

ISBN 978-1-5247-7037-2 (trade) — ISBN 978-1-5247-7038-9 (lib. bdg.)
ISBN 978-1-5247-7039-6 (ebook)

Printed in the United States of America

10 9 8 7 6 5 4 3 2 1

# A Colorful Christmas!

by Xiomara Nieves

Random House 🏠 New York

Frosty the Snowman
loves all the colors
at Christmas!

There is white,
fluffy snow.

There is a black
magic hat.

Frosty wears
a long red scarf.

Musicians in blue
uniforms play
instruments.

There are presents tied
with purple ribbons.

A man sells green

Christmas trees.

The woodland animals put orange ornaments on a tree.

There is a yellow star
on top of
a Christmas tree.

Frosty shares a pink
treat with his friends.

Here comes jolly
Santa Claus
with his reindeer.

Santa wears a red suit,
and his reindeer
are brown.
His sleigh is filled
with colorful gifts.

# There is a purple ball.

There is a blue train.

There is a brown
teddy bear.

There is a green robot.

Have a colorful
Christmas!

# Dear Parents:

Congratulations! Your child is taking the first steps on an exciting journey. The destination? Independent reading!

**STEP INTO READING**® will help your child get there. The program offers five steps to reading success. Each step includes fun stories and colorful art or photographs. In addition to original fiction and books with favorite characters, there are Step into Reading Non-Fiction Readers, Phonics Readers and Boxed Sets, Sticker Readers, and Comic Readers—a complete literacy program with something to interest every child.

## Learning to Read, Step by Step!

**Ready to Read   Preschool–Kindergarten**
• big type and easy words • rhyme and rhythm • picture clues
For children who know the alphabet and are eager to begin reading.

**Reading with Help   Preschool–Grade 1**
• basic vocabulary • short sentences • simple stories
For children who recognize familiar words and sound out new words with help.

**Reading on Your Own   Grades 1–3**
• engaging characters • easy-to-follow plots • popular topics
For children who are ready to read on their own.

**Reading Paragraphs   Grades 2–3**
• challenging vocabulary • short paragraphs • exciting stories
For newly independent readers who read simple sentences with confidence.

**Ready for Chapters   Grades 2–4**
• chapters • longer paragraphs • full-color art
For children who want to take the plunge into chapter books but still like colorful pictures.

**STEP INTO READING**® is designed to give every child a successful reading experience. The grade levels are only guides; children will progress through the steps at their own speed, developing confidence in their reading.

Remember, a lifetime love of reading starts with a single step!

*For Matt, my big little brother –C.B.C.*

RHUS39292

All rights reserved. Published in the United States by Random House Children's Books, a division of Penguin Random House LLC, 1745 Broadway, New York, NY 10019, and in Canada by Penguin Random House Canada Limited, Toronto.

Step into Reading, Random House, and the Random House colophon are registered trademarks of Penguin Random House LLC.

Visit us on the Web!
StepIntoReading.com
randomhousekids.com

Educators and librarians, for a variety of teaching tools, visit us at RHTeachersLibrarians.com

ISBN 978-1-5247-7037-2 (trade) — ISBN 978-1-5247-7038-9 (lib. bdg.)
ISBN 978-1-5247-7039-6 (ebook)

Printed in the United States of America

10 9 8 7 6 5 4 3 2 1

# SNOW DAY!

adapted by Courtney B. Carbone

illustrated by Fabio Laguna and Andrea Cagol

Random House 🏠 New York

A magician named
Professor Hinkle
came to school.
He had a funny bunny.

Professor Hinkle's tricks
did not work!
He threw away
his magic hat.

The school bell rang.

The kids ran outside.

They made a snowman
and named him Frosty!

He had a corncob pipe,
a button nose,
and two eyes
made out of coal.

A gust of winter wind
blew the magician's hat
through the air.
It landed on Frosty.

Frosty came to life!
"Happy birthday!"
he said with a smile.
The kids cheered.

Professor Hinkle took his magic hat back!

The bunny
returned the hat
to Frosty.
He came back to life!

Frosty was so much fun.

He danced and sang.

He led a parade

through town!

Suddenly, Frosty
began to melt!
He had to go
someplace cold.

A girl named Karen
found a train going north.

The train car was
great for Frosty.
But it was too cold
for Karen.

They got off the train
at the next stop.
Professor Hinkle had
followed them.

Frosty and Karen
needed to escape.
Frosty raced down a hill
with Karen on his back.

They went inside
a greenhouse,
where it was warm.
The magician found them.
He locked them inside!

"Oh, no!" Karen cried.
Frosty melted
into a puddle of water.

The bunny went
to get help.
Santa Claus came
to the rescue!

Santa unlocked the door.
A winter wind blew in
and froze the water.
Frosty came back
to life!

"Happy birthday!"
he said again.

Karen was so happy!

Santa took Karen home.
Frosty would go
to the North Pole
with Santa!

Frosty promised
to come back and visit.